Best Loved Stories

TOM SAWYER

by Mark Twain

Abridged edition

Victor and vanquished

"Tom!" No answer.

"Tom!" Silence.

"What's happened to that boy, I wonder? You, Tom!" The old lady pulled her spectacles down and looked over them, then put them up and looked out under them. No one. She looked under the bed, then went to the door and stood there, peering among the weeds in the garden. No Tom. So she raised her voice and shouted: "You, Tom!" and added: "I never saw anything like that boy!"

A slight noise made her turn, just in time to seize a small boy by the slack of his coat.

"I might have thought of that cupboard! What were you doing in there?"

"Nothing, Aunt Polly!"

"Nothing! Look at your hands and mouth! It's jam, and I've told you not to touch it. Hand me that switch, and I'll teach you to disobey me!"

The switch hovered in the air. The peril was desperate.

"Aunt Polly, look behind you!"

The old lady whirled round and as she did so the boy slipped away, clambered up the garden fence, slipped over it and vanished. When Aunt Polly had recovered from her surprise, she burst out laughing.

"The rascal! He always catches me off-guard, and I always end up laughing at him. And I always forgive him. I'm not doing my duty towards him, but I do hate to spank him. My poor sister left him to me when she died and told me to bring him up healthy and hardworking, but Tom hates work more than anything. I ought to be stricter with him and make him work tomorrow — that's Saturday. But he may as well enjoy himself today."

And Tom certainly did, that day, getting home just in time to help Jim, the small coloured boy, saw up wood; or rather he pretended to help, while Sid, his half-brother, a quiet, plodding lad, collected and stacked the wood. At supper Aunt Polly tried to discover whether Tom had been at school, but he managed to avoid the traps she set for him and slipped out of the house.

It was not yet dark, and Tom hurried on to the middle of the village. Suddenly he came across a boy larger than himself, a stranger.

The two boys stopped, face to face, and stared into each other's eyes without a word. At last Tom opened hostilities.

"I could lick you, if I wanted to. I could!"

"Try! Why don't you?"

The boys grabbed each other like cats, rolled in the dust, scratched and punched and pulled each other's hair, and covered themselves in dust and glory. Finally Tom managed to get astride his enemy and pin down his arms.

"Give in!" panted Tom.

"Give in," muttered the boy, half suffocated.

So Tom let go and the stranger moved off, dusting

8

his clothes and sobbing and, as he walked away, turning occasionally to threaten vengeance.

It was late when he reached home that night, and when he climbed in through the window he fell straight into Aunt Polly's arms.

When she saw the state his clothes were in, she decided it was more important than ever to give him a really serious punishment.

Next day, instead of having a holiday like all the other boys, he was to whitewash the whole of the garden fence.

Painting the fence

Everyone in St. Petersburg felt cheerful and smiling that sunny Saturday morning. Everyone except Tom Sawyer. When he appeared with a bucket of whitewash and a long-handled brush, his face looked melancholy and sad. A glance at the size of the fence made him feel even gloomier. Then, with a sigh, he set to work.

After a while he compared the work he had done, a tiny white strip, with the enormous area still waiting to be painted, and sat down feeling discouraged.

Wearily, Tom started work again, but when he saw his friend Ben Rogers, he started painting furiously. Ben came over and spoke to Tom, but Tom, who seemed completely absorbed in his work, made no reply. Ben was a little vexed.

9

"Well, I'm off to the river," he said. "But if you'd sooner stay here working, work away. You can't make me believe you're enjoying it!"

"I can't see why I shouldn't be enjoying it. D'you think a boy gets the chance of whitewashing such a beautiful fence every day? Well, does he?"

This kind of argument made things look different. Ben watched Tom moving the brush back and forward, standing back a step to see the effect, and then adding a touch here and there.

"Look, Tom," Ben said at last, "let me have a go."

Tom hesitated.

"I can't. Aunt Polly minds too much about her fence. I'm sorry, Ben, I just can't."

"Oh come on, Tom! Let me have a go. I'll really do it properly. I'd let you, if you asked me. Look, I'll give you . . . an apple!"

After a great deal more pleading, Tom let himself be persuaded and gave up his brush; and while the volunteer was working and sweating at the fence, Tom munched the apple and wondered how he could get other simpletons to work in his place.

He managed it. Every now and then a boy would stop to jeer and stay to work. By the time Ben was tired, Tom had sold the job to Billy Fisher, and halfway through the afternoon had grown rich: a dozen marbles, any number of corks and other objects had been exchanged for the privilege of painting.

10

Quite apart from doing good business, Tom had enjoyed himself, and the fence had been given three coats of whitewash. If he had not run out of whitewash, he would have made every boy in the village bankrupt; instead, he had to turn willing helpers away. When he went into the house at last, Aunt Polly was surprised to see him and thought he must be resting from his labours.

"How much of the work have you done?" she asked.

"It's all done, Aunt Polly," Tom said in an unconvincing tone.

"Tom, don't lie to me! You know I won't have it. Come now, tell the truth."

"It *is* the truth, Aunt Polly. It's really all done."

Aunt Polly felt so sceptical that she went out to see for herself. A fraction of what he claimed would have satisfied her, and when she saw the whole fence whitewashed, and given several careful coats at that, her amazement was unbounded. She turned to Tom delightedly.

"I'd never have believed it. But I've got to admit you can really work hard when you want to!" Then, to avoid overpraising him, she added: "The trouble is you want to so seldom. Run along and play, you've earned it. But don't be late back, or you'll catch it from me."

Tom made for the village square, a favourite meeting place for all the boys of St. Petersburg. As he passed Jeff Thatcher's house, he saw an unknown little girl in the garden; a pretty child with blue eyes and fair hair in pigtails, and Tom kept glancing furtively at her, until he was quite sure she had noticed him.

For a while he did balancing tricks on the pavement opposite the Thatchers' house, apparently concentrating on not putting a foot wrong. Then he started more ambitious acrobatics on the Thatchers' fence, while the little girl watched him secretly, making no move towards him.

For a while he carried on "showing off"; then, in the middle of a somersault, he glanced at the garden and saw that the little girl was going into the house.

When she was on the steps, Tom sighed heavily, but just as she was going inside, she turned and smiled at him. It was a sweet smile, and her whole expression was filled with admiration for Tom.

That smile kept Tom hanging about the fence till nightfall, but the little girl never appeared again. It was late when he gave up watching and walked home, his mind full of visions and dreams.

The Sunday school champion

The sun rose over a quiet world and its rays poured down on St. Petersburg like a blessing.

It was a splendid Sunday, but Tom was in no state to appreciate the beauties of nature. He had to learn five verses from the Bible by heart in time for

Sunday school that very morning. Of course, he had had all the week to learn them in, and Sid had known them days ago; but Tom had left it till the very last minute. Half an hour's work had little effect, because he kept getting distracted. And when his cousin Mary suggested hearing his verses, he had nothing to say.

"Oh, Tom, why won't you do your work?" said Mary. "Look, try your very best and learn the verses, and if you do, I'll give you something very nice."

"Oh, what?" said Tom, his curiosity aroused.

"I shan't tell you. But it's really nice."

"Right, I'll try!" And under the double pressure of curiosity and self-interest, he learnt the five verses by heart. Mary then gave him a penknife, which was blunt and had no point, but delighted Tom just the same; and when she gave him a basin of water and a piece of soap to wash with, he never even murmured a protest, as he usually did.

He went into the garden, put the basin on a bench and the soap into the water. Then he laid it beside the basin, turned back to the kitchen, pretending to dry himself. But Mary snatched away the towel.

"Oh Tom, for shame! Are you scared of water?"

Tom had nothing to answer to that. He went back to the garden, wetted his face with his fingertips and went back to the house. Mary was not deceived, and made him wash again in front of her. Then, still not satisfied, she turned back her own sleeves and finished the job herself. When she had done with him Tom was pale, clean, unrecognisable.

14

Washed and combed, Tom had to put on his Sunday clothes and his shoes. All this made him so uncomfortable and impatient that he burst out complaining that he always had to do what he disliked; but Mary stood firm and Tom had to make himself look like a neat, hateful town boy. Mary and Sid were ready in no time and the three of them set off for Sunday school in the village church.

In the church porch Tom hung back a little, and approached another boy.

"Hey, Bill, got a yellow ticket? Swap it for two white marbles?"

Bill agreed, and the business was settled. Tom hung about for another ten minutes, swapping tickets for treasures, and when he went into the church he had a number of tickets of various colours.

Tom's class was made up of rowdy youngsters who became bored and cross. No one really knew the lessons, but with promptings from the rest of the class everyone managed to collect a prize from the master, who was old and deaf: a blue ticket for every two verses recited from memory.

Ten blue tickets could be exchanged for a red one, and ten red tickets for a yellow one. For ten yellow tickets the prize was a Bible. But only the most careful managed to keep their tickets and only the most hardworking learnt enough verses, so that when a Bible was presented it was a memorable event.

The lesson was nearly over when Lawyer Thatcher came in, with an old gentleman and a little girl that Tom recognised at once.

The teacher presented the visitors to the school, which learnt that the old gentleman was Lawyer Thatcher's brother and a county judge. No one as important had ever been seen in St. Petersburg before and the teacher swelled with pride at the thought of his visiting the Sunday school.

Only one thing could have increased his delight: the chance to give someone the prize of a Bible, and to show off an outstanding pupil. But even the most diligent had not the right number of tickets. When all hope was lost, Tom suddenly stood up with a bunch of coloured tickets. This was a thunder-bolt out of a clear sky. The teacher was not expecting an application from Tom for the next ten years. But there was no getting around it — he had the right number of tickets. So Tom was taken to sit up with the judge, and the great news was announced. The boys were all eaten up with envy, and those who suffered most were those who realised too late that they themselves had contributed to Tom's glory by exchanging tickets for the wealth Tom had amassed in selling the privilege of whitewashing Aunt Polly's fence.

The teacher handed Tom the prize and introduced him to the judge.

"Two thousand verses is a very, very great many," said the judge. "And you'll never be sorry for the time you took to learn them. And now, you wouldn't mind telling me some of the things you've learned? What were the names of the first two Apostles?"

Tom blushed and looked down. The teacher held his breath. The whole Sunday school held its breath.

"David and Goliath!" cried Tom.

We will draw a veil over what happened next and hurry on to Monday morning.

On the way to school Tom met Huckleberry Finn, the poorest boy in the village and son of the local drunkard. Huck always wore ragged men's clothes, and could do exactly what he liked; no one made him wash or go to school. In other words, he was hated and feared by all the mothers in St. Petersburg, and loved and admired by all the boys.

"Hullo, Huckleberry! What's that you've got?" called Tom.

"Dead cat."

"My, he's pretty stiff! What's dead cats for, Huck?"

"It's for curing warts," said Huck. "D'you know what you do? You go to a cemetery when somebody that was wicked has been buried. At midnight the devils come and get him. You can't see them, but you can hear them. Then, when they're carrying off the corpse, you throw the cat at them and say: 'Devil follow corpse, cat follow devil, warts follow cat.' It always works and I'm going to try it tonight, when the devils come and fetch old Hoss Williams, who's just been buried."

"Look, Huck," said Tom excitedly. "Could I come with you?"

"Of course — if you ain't scared."

"Scared! Not likely."

Tom went off to the schoolhouse, where he strode in extraordinarily late. He flung himself into his seat with a business-like air.

Among ghosts and murderers

Tom's arrival was greeted by the master with: "Tom Sawyer, why on earth are you late today?"

Tom would have come out with a fib if he had not caught sight of some blonde pigtails he recognised at once. The new girl was sitting on her own, and the only empty seat on the girls' side of the classroom was on the bench beside her.

18

"I stopped to talk to Huck Finn!" he said.

The master was astounded, and the children wondered if Tom had gone mad, since no one sane would admit to such a thing.

"Tom Sawyer," stammered the master, "I've never heard such an insolent admission. Go and sit with the girls, and let that be a lesson to you!"

It looked as if the children's giggles had disconcerted Tom, but in fact he had coloured up with emotion at being told to sit among the girls, which meant next to *that* particular girl. He sat down on the very edge of the bench, while she drew away to the other end.

Tom started drawing on his slate, keeping his left hand over it. At first the girl pretended not to notice, then she showed signs of curiosity; and at last she poked her head forward to see. Tom showed her his masterpiece: a house with a pitched roof and a chimney with a corkscrew of smoke coming out of it.

The little girl whispered: "It's lovely! Oh, I wish I could draw!"

Tom offered to teach her, and after a few minutes and a great deal of whispering they were old friends. Tom discovered that her name was Becky Thatcher, that the judge was her father and that she was going to stay in St. Petersburg for a long time.

He started writing on his slate again, hiding what he wrote, and Becky asked to see it.

"If you promise never to tell anyone as long as you live."

"I promise. No one'll ever know, not in a million years!"

Tom took his hand off the slate and showed her the words: 'I love you'. Becky blushed, and Tom took her hand. "Would you like us to be engaged?" he asked.

"I expect so, but I don't know. What's it like?"

Tom was just going to answer when he felt himself seized by the ear and dragged back to his own seat, while the whole class roared with laughter. The master stood over him for a moment without speaking, then went back to his desk, leaving Tom with an aching ear and a jubilant heart.

At the noon break, Tom went over to Becky.

"Remember, when you're engaged you go to school together and home together, and you've always got to choose me in games and I've got to choose you."

"How lovely!" cried Becky.

"It's ever so jolly!" said Tom. "Why, Amy Lawrence and I . . ."

Becky's eyes told Tom he had made a mistake. "So you were engaged to Amy, were you? And I thought I was the only one . . ."

"But Becky, I don't care about Amy in the least!"

"I don't believe you, Tom. I expect you've been engaged to every girl in the school! Go away, I never want to see you again, Tom Sawyer!"

Tom tried to win her round with soft words, but it was no good.

When lessons were over Tom went off to hide in the woods on Cardiff Hill. He felt melancholy, and the place suited his mood.

After supper, Tom went to bed but lay awake, feeling restless and impatient.

At last, the church clock struck eleven. A moment later Tom was dressed and had dropped out of the window on to the woodshed roof; he crawled along it and then jumped down to the ground, and waited in the darkness for Huck. When he turned up, the two of them vanished into the night.

In half an hour they were in the tall grass of the cemetery.

A faint wind moaned in the trees and Tom thought with terror that it might be the spirits of the dead complaining of being disturbed.

Almost at once they found the newly-dug grave they were looking for and hid behind a tree a few feet away. Then they waited in silence for what seemed a long time.

Suddenly Tom seized Huck's arm and murmured: "Sh . . . can't you hear?" and clung to Huck.

"Oh Lord, Tom, they're coming. It must be them . . . what shall we do?"

"They won't hurt us, because we haven't done anything wrong. You'll see. If we keep still, they may not even notice us."

"I'll try and keep still, Tom, but I'm shaking so."

The boys bent their heads together and scarcely breathed. From the far end of the graveyard they heard the muffled sound of voices.

Vague figures approached them in the darkness, swinging an old lantern that spangled the ground with light.

"Oh Lord, Tom, I can see three devils! They're humans! One of them's old Muff Potter!"

"Muff Potter? No . . . it can't be!"

"So it is. And I can tell you another of the voices — it's Injun Joe's."

The three men stopped by Hoss Williams's grave, a few feet from the boys, and Joe and the old man started digging. For a moment the lantern lit up the third man's face: it was young Dr. Robinson.

For a time there was no noise but that of the spades removing earth, then a spade struck the coffin with a dull thud. The men lifted it out of the ground and Potter prized it open with his knife.

Injun Joe, meantime, had gone up to the doctor.

"Out with another five," he said, "or here it stays!"

"What? I've paid you in advance and paid you enough."

"Oh, no, it's not enough. I've an old score to settle with the Robinsons. Your father had me jailed as a vagrant and I swore to get even. Now I've got you!" And he threatened the doctor with his fist. Dr. Robinson hurled himself on Joe and knocked him down at Muff Potter's feet; Potter dropped the knife and leaped at the doctor, who picked up a shovel and felled him with it.

Joe got up and seized the knife. He plunged it into the doctor's heart; the doctor fell on top of Muff, pouring blood over him. He gasped and lay still; and Injun Joe robbed the body, put the knife in the unconscious Muff Potter's hand and sat down on the coffin. After a while Potter began to stir. He got up, glanced at the knife and at the body, and then said with a groan: "Lord, Joe, what happened?"

"You killed him," said Joe.

"I don't remember hitting him. I'm all in a muddle. Joe, did I really hit him? I didn't mean to. He was so young and good — it's terrible!"

"No good crying over spilt milk," said Joe. "This is what happened. He hit you with the spade and knocked you down. You got up again, and when he was going to hit you again you jammed the knife into his chest. Then you both fell flat on the ground."

"I didn't know what I was doing, I swear it! Joe, you won't tell, will you? Promise you won't?" And old Muff Potter fell on his knees before the murderer, clasping his hands in prayer.

"I won't talk, but now we must get out," said Injun Joe, and they ran from the place, leaving a lidless coffin and an open grave, a blood-stained knife, two shovels and two terrified boys.

The Mississippi pirates

Tom and Huck ran back to the village as fast as their legs would carry them. Before parting, for fear of Injun Joe's revenge, they swore a solemn oath to say nothing of what they had seen in the graveyard.

It was about midday that the crime was discovered, and as Muff Potter's knife was found beside the doctor's body, the sheriff put out a search for him. Within a few hours the old man was caught and, in spite of his protests, charged with Dr. Robinson's murder and with violating Williams's grave. Injun Joe accused him, and Potter was imprisoned, awaiting trial. Nobody doubted that he would hang.

Only Tom and Huck could save the innocent man, but who would believe them? And besides, they had sworn to be silent. But their consciences tormented them, and Tom in particular found it hard to get to sleep and suffered horrible nightmares.

One morning at breakfast Sid remarked, in front of Aunt Polly: "Tom, you've been tossing about and talking in your sleep and keeping me awake."

"You're pale, Tom," said Aunt Polly. "Maybe you're sickening for something. I've read about a new medicine which is supposed to cure everything. I'll buy a bottle today."

After lunch Tom had his first spoonful of Painkiller and Aunt Polly watched anxiously for the result. Before the medicine, Tom had been gloomy, and pale, but after it he suddenly seemed to come alive again, and Aunt Polly stopped worrying.

After a while she realized that Tom, for the first time in his life, was enjoying medicine, in fact he asked for it so often that she told him to help himself and stop bothering her.

Very likely no one would have noticed that Tom was pouring the stuff into a crack in the sitting room floor, if one day Aunt Polly's cat, Peter, had not come along while he was doing so.

Peter came up to Tom and sniffed at the spoonful of medicine, looking as if he would like to try it. Tom tried to dissuade him, and when Peter begged for a taste said: "D'you really want it? You can have it if you really want it, but no complaints later!"

Tom opened Peter's mouth and poured the Painkiller into it. The poor creature leapt a couple of yards into the air, howled furiously and dashed round the room, banging the furniture. Then he rose on his hind legs and started dancing about in a frenzy of delight.

Aunt Polly arrived to see Peter's final jumps, after which he leapt through the window, knocking a vase of flowers over on the way.

"Now," thundered Aunt Polly, "just tell me why you treated Peter like that."

"I did it because he hasn't got an aunt!"

"What have aunts got to do with it?"

"Plenty. Because if he'd had an aunt she'd have burnt his inside out for him, just as if he'd been human!"

Aunt Polly felt a pang of remorse. What was cruel to a cat might be equally cruel to a boy. She began to soften and said gently: "I was trying to do my best for you, Tom."

"I know, and I was doing my best for Peter . . ."

"Now, Tom, you're going to make me cross again! Get along to school, or you'll be late."

Tom reached school before it was time to start and broke into a war-dance, chased the other boys, leaped over the fence and kept glancing furtively at Becky, to see if she was noticing him.

"Some people never stop showing off," she said.

Tom crept away, crestfallen and despairing.

All during the day he thought of his sorrows, and decided that he would run away from home. When lessons were over he made for the river, where he met his friend Joe Harper.

Joe was no less sad and bitter than Tom. That

morning his mother had punished him severely for drinking some cream he had never even tasted.

Joe was well able to sympathise with Tom's troubles, and they swore to be brothers all their lives. They began to make plans for the future, and de-

cided that to become pirates was the best career they could choose.

Then Huckleberry Finn agreed to join them, all careers being the same to him.

Jackson Island, a well-wooded, uninhabited island in the Mississippi about three miles from St. Petersburg, was chosen as their base. It was far enough from the shore and seemed an ideal hiding-place.

A small raft lay on the river bank and at sunset the three boys, laden with provisions and weapons (a boiled ham from Aunt Polly's larder, and some wooden swords), set sail under the black pirate flag. Tom gave orders the crew pretended to obey.

"Luff, and bring her to the wind!"

"Aye, aye, sir!"

It was dark when the raft landed on the sandy beach of Jackson Island and the boys waded ashore. They went about fifty yards into the woods, lit a fire under a big tree and fried some bacon which they ate with half the bread they had brought. Filled with contentment, they all declared that nothing would ever make them go back to civilization.

"What would the boys say if they could see us," said Joe.

"Why, they'd just die of envy, wouldn't they, Huck?" said Tom.

"I expect so," said Huck. "Anyway, it's fine for me. I couldn't ask for anything better. At home I don't generally get enough to eat, and here people can't come and bother me, either."

"It's just the life for me," said Tom. "No need to go to school, or wash, or do anything stupid like that."

Gradually conversation died and the three boys began to feel sleepy. Huck was the first to sleep, but Tom and Joe found it harder. They said their prayers to themselves, lying down, since there was no one to make them say them aloud and kneeling. In fact they had meant not to say them at all, but were afraid to go to such lengths of piracy as that, for fear of calling down a special thunderbolt from heaven.

The pirates awoke to the dawn chorus and spent the morning exploring the island. With an improvised hook and line Huck caught some fish for breakfast, and they all agreed that they had never tasted anything as delicious. After breakfast they rested, and then went back to exploring.

Late in the afternoon they saw a small steam ferryboat, with a large number of skiffs around it, drifting with the current. Suddenly a jet of white smoke burst from the ferryboat's side, followed by the sullen boom of cannon fire.

"Someone's drowned," said Huck. "They fire into the water to make the body come up. I wish I knew who was drowned."

They were watching the ferryboat when Tom suddenly had his idea.

"Boys," he cried. "I know who's drowned! It's us!"

Then the boat disappeared and the three of them,

feeling jubilant, tried to imagine the scenes of public mourning and what would be said in memory of them. But their excitement was shortlived. Tom and Joe could not help thinking of the way their families must be feeling.

When darkness fell, the three boys crowded together to rest. Huck was the first to fall asleep, and then Joe. Tom stayed motionless for a while, watching them, then he got up and went to look for the thin white bark of a sycamore.

He knelt by the fire and with difficulty wrote something on two pieces of bark. One he put in his pocket, the other he left beside Huck. Then he left the camp and ran to the island's pebbly shore.

Return to civilization

A few minutes later Tom was swimming across the river, and managed to get to the bank quite easily and quickly.

He walked inland and used unfrequented roads to reach the fence behind his own house. He climbed it and approached the only window that was still lit up — Aunt Polly's room. In it, besides Aunt Polly, were Joe Harper's mother, Sid and Mary.

Tom crept in without a sound. In the passage he moved along on all fours and in a few minutes had slithered under Aunt Polly's bed, which stood near her door.

"He wasn't a bad boy at all," Aunt Polly was saying. "Only mischievous and full of mad ideas. Like a colt . . . But he never meant any harm . . ."

Aunt Polly's words, and some further remarks of Mary's moved Tom to tears. Their sorrow upset him so much that he longed to rush over to embrace them; but he managed to control himself and stayed listening where he was.

He learned that the boys were thought to have been drowned while bathing, and that even if their bodies were not recovered by Saturday evening they were to be commemorated in a funeral service on Sunday. Tom shuddered.

Mrs. Harper left and when Sid and Mary had gone to bed, Aunt Polly knelt down and prayed for Tom

so touchingly and lovingly that Tom was weeping long before she had finished.

He had to wait a long time after she had gone to bed, because she was too heartbroken to drop off to sleep.

He was just going to put the sycamore bark by the candlestick when something occurred to him; a splendid idea that made him put it back in his pocket, kiss Aunt Polly, and creep out of the house.

He went to the ferry landing, found the boat he was looking for and was soon rowing.

The current carried him to Jackson Island, where he dived into the water. The boat continued on its way and vanished into the darkness.

He went back to the camp at dawn, arriving just in time to hear Joe say: "He'll be back. Tom won't desert. He's up to something, and I wonder what it is. The writing says he'll be back for breakfast."

"And so he is," said Tom, stepping grandly into the camp. A breakfast of bacon and fish was soon ready, and while they ate Tom told them of his adventures, explained the plan he had in mind, and urged them to approve it.

That day, a Thursday, had started heroically — but ended in a very different atmosphere.

After supper of fish and turtles' eggs, Huck took out his pipe, lit it and started smoking.

Tom and Joe wanted to try as well, and Huck produced two clay pipes, filled them, lit them, and held them out to the other pirates. Tom and Joe started smoking — cautiously, because the tobacco's flavour was unpleasant and made them cough.

"It's easy, isn't it! If only I'd known, I'd have started sooner!" said Tom.

"Me too," said Joe. "There's nothing to it. In fact I bet I could smoke a whole day without feeling bad."

Joe suddenly got up and, dead pale, staggered away from the camp and into the wood. "I've lost my knife. I think I'd better find it before it's dark . . ." he said.

"I'll help you," said Tom, gritting his teeth. "You go that way and I'll go to the spring . . ."

Huck waited an hour. Then, feeling lonely, he went to look for the others, and found them, far from each other and fast asleep. Something told him that if they had had any trouble they had got rid of it. Huck said nothing, but he never offered them another smoke.

Next day proved a gloomy one, for there was a violent thunderstorm and Jackson Island was drenched in heavy rain. But the sun soon came out again and the pirates were able to go back to fishing, mock battles, and looking for turtles' eggs.

Back in St. Petersburg it was a sorrowful Saturday. The Harpers and Aunt Polly's family were profoundly sad, and other people went about their daily business talking little and sighing a great deal.

On Sunday morning, when Sunday school was over, the church bell began to toll and everyone crowded into church for the funeral service. Aunt Polly, Sid, Mary and the Harpers sat in the front row.

Hymns were sung, and the clergyman spoke of the lost boys' virtues and promise so movingly that everyone in the congregation felt guilty at having been so obstinately blind to them, seeing only their failings and flaws; and gradually, as the sermon proceeded, not only the mourners but the whole company broke down and wept.

While this pathetic tale was being told, the church door creaked, and the clergyman stopped, staring transfixed over the heads of the congregation. First one, then two pairs of eyes followed his, until at last the whole congregation rose and stared, while the three dead boys came marching up the aisle.

The boys were clasped in the arms of their relations and for a while nothing was heard but their exclamations. Then the minister started up a hymn of thanksgiving, which made everyone forget the punishment the pirates so richly deserved.

A noble gesture

Aunt Polly was far too happy at finding her Tom safe and sound to put much energy into punishments. She reproached him, though, for not having let her know he was alive.

On Monday morning Tom went back to school, and it was clear at once that everyone, large or small, was gazing admiringly at him and Joe (since Huck never went to school, he could not share in this admiration). The one-time pirates had to tell of their adventures, but they never really reached the end of them, because as they went along they found themselves imagining too many incidents ever to finish.

It was when they talked about smoking — bending the truth just a little — that they reached the peak of their glory. Tom decided that he could manage quite well without Becky.

Little by little, in fact, Becky wàs approaching him. She started skipping and chasing the other girls, squealing and giggling whenever she caught one, but strangely enough this happened only when she was near Tom's little group.

Tom realized what she was up to, but he pretended not to have noticed she was there.

When Tom got home at lunch time, Aunt Polly's first words told him that he could expect no cheer from her.

"Tom, I've a good mind to skin you alive," she said. "I went to Mrs. Harper's. Joe told her that you were here that evening, and saw and heard everything that went on. You were just enjoying yourself at our expense!"

"I know I was wrong, Aunt Polly, but I didn't do it on purpose. And I didn't come to enjoy myself at your expense. I swear I didn't."

"What did you come for, then?"

"To tell you not to worry, because we hadn't been

drowned. I'd written a message on some bark, saying we'd gone to be pirates."

When Tom had gone to school, Aunt Polly got out the ragged jacket he had worn as a pirate. She looked in the pockets and found the piece of bark.

She read the message that had been meant for her and, deeply moved, said to herself: "Now I can forgive the boy everything, anything at all."

Near the school Tom met Becky and he said impulsively: "I wasn't nice to you this morning and I'm sorry. Let's be friends, Becky . . ."

Becky stopped and stared scornfully at him.

"I'll thank you to keep out of my way, Mr. Tom Sawyer," she said. "I never want to see you again and I'm never going to speak to you!"

He was furiously angry, and made rude remarks to her. Becky answered in kind and Tom's heart was filled with bitterness.

Then, to avoid him, Becky went into the classroom. She was alone, and went over to the master's desk. Mr. Dobbins, the master, had an ambition to become a doctor, and every free moment he had he spent studying a large mysterious book which he kept in the desk. No one had ever managed to get a close look at it; everyone longed to see it, but no one ever got the chance.

That day, as Becky approached the desk, she saw that the key was in the lock, and she took out the book and started looking through it.

She was busy looking at a large coloured illustration of the human body when a shadow fell across the page. It was Tom Sawyer, who had crept up silently and was now looking at the picture as well. Becky slammed the book shut, and in doing so tore the illustration across the middle.

She put the book back in the desk, turned the key and burst into tears of shame and anger.

"Tom Sawyer, you're a horrid boy, creeping up and spying on people!"

"How could I know you were here?" said Tom.

"You ought to be ashamed of yourself! Now you'll go and tell on me, and I'll be whipped!"

Soon afterwards the master arrived and lessons began. While the children were working on their own, Mr. Dobbins opened his desk, took out the book and started reading.

Just at that moment the master saw the page. He shouted: "Who tore this book?" No one answered, so he questioned each child in turn, looking for signs of guilt . . .

When Mr. Dobbins had questioned all the boys, he went on to the girls.

"Amy Lawrence?" No. "Grace Miller?" Another no.

"Rebecca Thatcher . . . (Tom looked at her and saw that she was pale with terror) . . . Did you tear the book? . . . Did you? Come now, answer me!"

An idea flashed into Tom's mind. He leapt up and cried: "I tore it, sir! I did!"

The entire school turned and stared, astounded.

Tom walked firmly up to the desk to take his punishment.

The gratitude and admiration he read in Becky's eyes made up for even a hundred strokes.

And Tom himself was quite indifferent to them. He was even quite unruffled when Mr. Dobbins kept him in for two hours after lessons, because he knew that Becky would be waiting for him outside.

That evening when he went to bed he thought up plans of revenge on Mr. Dobbins. But happier thoughts soon took over and as he fell asleep he could still hear Becky's last words: "Oh Tom, how could you be so noble?"

Hero of St. Petersburg

Tom was not the only one to want vengeance on Mr. Dobbins. As the holidays drew nearer, the schoolmaster grew sterner. He wanted his school to do well in the exams, and so his cane was kept busy, hurting horribly, because although he was bald and wore a wig, his arm was still powerful.

The last days of term passed painfully. Finally the boys agreed on joint action to get their own back for what they were suffering.

The plot looked likely to succeed because before the 'examination' evening Mr. Dobbins always had a secret drink in his room, and got himself pretty well fuddled.

The great occasion arrived. Town dignitaries and parents sat on benches, and Mr. Dobbins sat in a large chair on a raised platform, with his blackboard behind him. It was clear that he had been drinking.

On his left, on a temporary platform, sat the pupils who were going to take part in the evening's exercises, all dressed in their best.

The exercises began. A tiny boy got an exaggerated round of applause, and was followed by a little girl lisping 'Mary had a little lamb'. Tom Sawyer then stepped forward and confidently started on 'Give me liberty or give me death' but broke down in the middle and had to stop.

Mr. Dobbins then went to the blackboard and began to draw a map of America, with which to exercise the geography class. But he made a poor show with his unsteady hand, and titters arose in the hall.

He rubbed the map out and started again, but things went worse than ever and the titters grew more pronounced. The map then seemed to improve, yet the laughter, to his surprise, grew more pronounced. Mr. Dobbins could not guess why.

From the ceiling, just above his head, through a trapdoor to the attic, a cat, tied round the haunches with string, was slowly descending. The poor creature kept clawing at the string, then at the air.

Down, down she came, to within a few inches of Mr. Dobbins's head, as he stood drawing at the blackboard. The tittering grew louder and louder.

Then suddenly the cat grabbed the teacher's wig in her desperate claws, and was snatched up to the attic in a moment.

What a splendid sight met the audience's eyes! Under the strong lights Mr. Dobbins's head gleamed brilliantly!

The meeting broke up and the school year ended merrily. The boys were avenged, the holidays had come, and it was time to make plans.

Tom got measles, and for two weeks lay a prisoner, interested in nothing.

When he got up he found everything and everybody extraordinarily melancholy.

The sleepy atmosphere was stirred at last by the murder trial, which immediately became the most absorbing topic of conversation. Tom's conscience was uneasy; the terrible secret of the murder was a misery, and every reference to it sent a shudder to his heart.

When he was alone with Huck he felt the need to share his distress and be reassured that Huck had remained silent.

"Of course I haven't talked, Tom," said Huck. "I'll never tell anyone. Why, we wouldn't be alive two days if that got out!"

The evening before the trial Tom and Huck did as they had often done before — they went to the back of the jail and gave Muff Potter some tobacco and matches. The old man's gratitude for their gifts had always troubled them, but this time it cut deeper.

They felt cowardly and treacherous when Potter said; "You've been mighty good to me and I'll never forget it. It's good to see friendly faces when you're in trouble!"

Tom went home miserable, and next day hung round the courtroom. Things were going badly for poor Muff Potter.

Injun Joe confirmed what he had said before: Potter had not only helped the doctor to rob a grave (doctors in those days had to do this if they wanted to make experiments in anatomy, and if they were caught paid dearly for it), but he had also committed the more terrible crime of murder.

Before the last day of the trial, Tom stayed out late.

Next morning the courthouse was packed to hear the sentence. Potter, in chains, was seated where everyone could stare at him.

When the judge was seated, counsel for the prosecution said firmly: "The oaths of citizens in this courthouse have proved without a shadow of a doubt that the crime was committed by the unhappy prisoner at the bar . . ."

A dreadful silence fell, and counsel for the defence rose. "Your Honour, at the opening of this trial we said that our client did this deed under the influence of drink. We have changed our mind. Call Thomas Sawyer."

A puzzled amazement showed on every face in the courthouse, including Potter's. Everyone stared

42

at Tom as he rose and took his place on the stand. He looked badly scared, and his voice shook as he took the oath.

"Thomas Sawyer, where were you on the seventeenth of June, about the hour of midnight? Speak up, and don't be afraid."

Tom glanced at Injun Joe's iron face, and his tongue almost failed him.

"In the graveyard, near Hoss Williams's grave."

"Tell us everything that happened."

Tom began, haltingly at first; but as he warmed to his subject the words flowed more easily.

All eyes were fixed on him. The audience hung on his words, fascinated by the terrible tale, and emotion reached its height when Tom said: "And as soon as Muff Potter fell, Injun Joe jumped with the knife and . . ." Crash! Injun Joe sprang for a window and vanished, proving the truth of Tom's tale.

Tom was a hero once more, but if his days were full of glory, his nights were full of terror. Injun Joe appeared in all his dreams. No one knew where he had vanished to. A price was put on his head, the countryside scoured, and at last it was decided that he must have left the state. No more was said of him.

The slow days drifted on, each slightly less anxious than the one before it. Even Tom began to forget.

There comes a time in every boy's life when he suddenly longs to go out and dig for treasure. This desire came upon Tom one day, and he went to find Huckleberry Finn. Huck was always ready to take part in anything that offered entertainment, and he had plenty of time to spare.

"Where'll we dig?" he asked.

"Oh, almost anywhere," said Tom airily.

"Why, is it hid all around?"

"No, indeed it ain't," said Tom. "It's hid in special places, Huck — sometimes on islands, sometimes in rotten chests under an old dead tree, just where the shadow falls at midnight. But mostly under the floor in haunted houses. We shan't try a desert island, but there's an old haunted house up the Still-House branch. All we need is a pick and shovel."

These they found, and set out on their tramp to the haunted house. Near it they found a dead tree, and decided it would do.

They worked and sweated for half an hour. No result. They toiled for another half hour. Still no result.

"Is treasure always buried as deep as this, Tom?" said Huck.

"Sometimes, but not always. Maybe we've got the wrong tree."

They changed their position and started digging again, but with no more success.

"I think we're wrong again," Tom said. "There can't be any hidden treasure here. I tell you what, Huck, we'll go to the haunted house!"

"Oh no, Tom! I don't like haunted houses! I'd die

of fright if I saw a ghost wrapped in a sheet, and I think you would too."

"Yes, I would, Huck, but ghosts only walk at night and as we'll be digging in the daytime they won't hurt us, really they won't."

The treasure hunters in trouble

When they came to the haunted house, something in its silence, as it lay under the hot sun, struck them as strange and horrible, and they felt frightened of going inside it. But they went cautiously up to the door, peered inside and saw a room with weeds growing up through the floor, peeling walls, broken windows and a crumbling staircase. And cobwebs everywhere.

With thudding hearts they crept inside, whispering to each other, their ears cocked for the slightest sound, ready to take to their heels.

Upstairs they found the same neglect, and were just about to leave when Tom suddenly stood stock still and made Huck a sign to be quiet.

"What is it?" Huck murmured, pale with fear. Then he whispered: "Ghosts! . . . Quick, let's go!"

"Stop! They're coming straight to the door."

The two boys flung themselves down on the floor and lay waiting in terror, peering through the cracks between the boards.

Two men came into the house, and each boy

thought: "One's the deaf-mute Spaniard who's been into town once or twice lately. The other I've never seen before." The Spaniard wore glasses with green lenses and a *sombrero*. The other man was a ragged, evil-looking fellow.

As they came in, this second man was talking in a low voice. The pair sat down on the floor, with their backs to the wall, and he went on speaking.

"No, I've thought it over and it's too dangerous," he said.

"Dangerous?" grunted the Spaniard, to the boys' amazement. "You're a coward! What's more dangerous than what we did down there?"

The voice was Injun Joe's.

"Look, wait for me to send for you. I'll go and have another look. Then we'll do the job you call dangerous. And then we'll be off to Texas."

"Right, I'll go. But what shall we do with the money that's left?"

"No good bringing it with us now. Six hundred and fifty dollars in silver's quite a weight. We must hide it better, though, because this place isn't safe."

The second man agreed and took a heavy bag from under a stone. From it he took a handful of coins, then handed the rest to Joe, who was kneeling in a corner digging with his knife.

The two boys forgot their fears. They had never seen so much money.

"Hey, there's a box buried here . . . I've made a hole in it . . . Let's see what's in it . . ." Injun Joe put his hand into the hole and drew it out full of gold coins.

"Here's something we must do at once," cried Joe's companion, wildly excited. Above, Tom and Huck were just as thrilled as the men. "I saw an old pick and a shovel over there," he said, and went to fetch the boys' tools.

Joe took the pick and began to dig. Soon the box was dug up.

When they had opened the box, the two men gazed at the treasure for a while. Then Joe said: "Well, there's thousands of dollars. It's always been said that Murrel's gang worked round here, and this proves it."

"Now we've got it, we shan't have to do that other job . . ."

Joe frowned. "You don't know me. I'm not interested in the money this time. It's a matter of revenge."

"All right. But what shall we do with this money? Bury it again?"

"Yes." (Enormous jubilation upstairs.) "No, we shan't!" (Enormous disappointment upstairs.) "I forgot. There was fresh earth on this pick. What's a pick and shovel doing here, anyway? And where's the people that brought them here?" (Terror upstairs.) "If we bury the treasure again they may come back and see newly-dug soil. We'll take it to my place."

"You're right. Where are you going to take it, to number one?"

"No, to number two, under the cross. Number one isn't safe."

Soon after this the two men crept out and set off towards the river with their precious box. Tom and Huck stared after them until they were out of sight, but made no attempt to follow. They crept out of the house and started for home.

They said little, but each cursed the moment they had flung down the pick and shovel. If they had only held on to the tools, Injun Joe would have suspected nothing and the gold and silver would have stayed in the house.

There was another possibility, though. When he came to St. Petersburg for his revenge they could follow the fake Spaniard to 'number two', wherever that might be. But while they were discussing this, a terrible thought struck Tom.

"Revenge? But who's Joe got it in for? It can't be us, can it?"

Huck nearly fainted at the thought, but Tom (though inwardly trembling) boldly maintained that now they were on the alert they need never be caught by Joe and his companion. In fact, they would try and catch the ruffians themselves, by finding out where 'number two' was. Tom and Huck started planning seriously.

Huck at last had an idea which Tom agreed with. 'Number two' must be the number of a room in an inn. And as there were two inns in St. Petersburg, they decided to have a look at once.

In the better of the two inns Tom found that room number two had been let for some time to a young lawyer. In the other, room number two was always locked and no one knew who rented it.

Tom and Huck decided to keep a watch on the inn.

On the third evening Tom decided to get into the mysterious room. He waited until all the inn lights had been put out, then crept inside while Huck stood guard on the road.

Huck waited for a long time, then heard Tom rush past him calling breathlessly: "Run, run!"

The pair of them never paused until they reached a safe place on the outskirts of the village.

"It was horrible!" said Tom. "The door of the room wasn't locked so I went in. I practically trod on Injun Joe! He was asleep on the floor. Luckily he didn't wake up."

"Did you see the box, Tom?"

"No. But we know where it is and we'll keep watch every night."

"I'll keep watch for a year, if I have to. If I see them going out with the box, I'll come and wake you."

"Right. Miaow like a cat and throw a stone at the window."

What Huck Finn did

The first thing Tom heard next morning was good news: Judge Thatcher's family had returned from their holiday the previous evening.

He went straight over to Becky's and spent the day with her. Becky asked her mother if they might have a picnic the next day, and she said they could. Before sunset everyone had been invited.

Excitement kept Tom awake until late, but Huck failed to appear, miaowing like a cat. Day dawned at last and all the youngsters turned up at Becky's.

The river ferryboat had been hired for the picnic and it stopped at the mouth of a woody hollow three miles from the town. Everyone landed, and soon the forests were echoing with shouts and laughter. Gradually the wanderers, feeling hungry, straggled back to camp for lunch.

After the feast somebody shouted: "Who's ready for the cave?"

Everybody was. Candles were produced, and there was a general scamper up the hill. The opening of the cave was high up the hill, a massive, unbarred oak door.

The candles were lit and everyone filed into the main avenue, where the flickering lights dimly showed the high rock walls almost meeting about sixty feet above. This main avenue was not more than eight or ten feet wide. Every few steps other narrower crevices branched out from it, for McDougal's cave was a vast labyrinth of crooked passages that ran into each other and led nowhere.

People said you might wander through it for days without finding the end of the cave.

The procession walked along the main gallery, then groups and couples began to slip aside into branch avenues and to take each other by surprise where the corridors met again. Gradually the groups came straggling back to the mouth of the cave, amazed to find they had lost track of time and night was nearly on them. The ferryboat bell had been clanging for half an hour. But when the boat pushed out into the river no one except the captain cared how much time had been lost.

Huck was already on watch when the ferryboat's lights went glinting past the wharf.

Ten o'clock struck. Lights began to go out and footsteps were no longer heard. The village was asleep, but Huck kept watch.

Eleven o'clock came, and Huck began to feel weary. Was there any point in watching? Why not turn in? He yawned, but stayed where he was. A little later he heard a sound: the inn door was opening. Huck stood in the shadows.

A second later two men brushed past him, and one seemed to have something under his arm. It must be that box! He decided to follow them. What was the point of calling Tom now? They would get away with the box forever.

Cat-like, Huck followed the two men. They turned into a path that led up Cardiff hill. "They must be going to the old quarry," thought Huck.

But they never stopped at the quarry. Where were they going? Huck sighed with relief. "Maybe they're going to bury it," he thought. "Well, let them. It won't be hard to find."

He heard a very low voice — Injun Joe's — say:

"Damn her, she's got company! There's lights on, though it's late."

"Yes, she must have visitors. Better give it up."

Huck recognised the voice as well; it was the second man's.

"Give it up? What about my revenge? Her husband was justice of the peace and had me put in jail as a vagrant. Then he died so I couldn't get my own back. But I'll take it out on the widow, that I will!"

Huck's heart heaved. So this was Joe's revenge!

He realised the two men were waiting for the guests to leave before doing their worst; so, without a sound, he dashed as fast as he could to the Welshman's house, where he banged on the door.

The door opened, and Huck told the Welshman and his stout sons what was happening.

Three minutes later the old man and his sons, well armed, were up the hill. Huck went with them, then hid behind a great boulder. A seemingly endless silence followed, then a sudden shot. This was too much for Huck. He sprang up and sped down the hill as fast as his legs would carry him.

At dawn next day Huck was back at the Welshman's. When he knocked, the door was opened at once, and he was greeted like an old friend and told what had happened in the night. Thanks to Huck, the villains had been put to flight before they could carry out their plan.

As they ran they had dropped a bulky package, burglar's tools.

Soon afterwards the widow Douglas turned up to thank those who had saved her. But the old Welshman broke in on her thanks.

"There's someone you owe much more to than you do to me and my sons," he said. "If it weren't for him . . ." and he told her just what had happened.

As he was finishing his story, news of another sensation arrived: Tom and Becky were lost in McDougal's cave!

Tom and Huck find 'number two'

What had happened to Tom and Becky? They went along the dark passages with the rest, and presently began playing hide-and-seek in the side avenues. This went on until they were weary, and they moved on to a place where a stream of water had trickled over a ledge. Beyond it Tom found a steep natural staircase between narrow walls of rock.

The explorer awoke in Tom and he called Becky to follow him. They started off up the steps.

It led them to a large cave full of stalactites, then on to a passage and an even larger one, with a splendid spring in the centre of it. Further on, Tom found an underground lake so large that its shape was lost in the darkness. He wanted to explore its shores but thought it best to rest awhile first.

"I wonder how long we've been down here," Becky said. "We'd better start back. Can you find the way, Tom? I'd hate to be lost here!"

They started off down a passage, but after a while Tom realised that everything about it was new. He looked everywhere for something familiar, but at last began to try passages at random, desperately hoping to find the right one. At one point he shouted, and the echo of his shout went through the empty cave.

"Oh, don't do it again, Tom!" said Becky. "It's too horrid."

"It is horrid, but I'd better, Becky. They *might* hear us," and he shouted again.

That 'might' terrified Becky even more than the shouts. She sank to the ground and burst into such desperate sobs that Tom sat down beside her and put his arms round her, trying to give her courage; then he started blaming himself for having got her into this terrible situation, and this had a better effect. Becky made an effort and rose to her feet; she said she would try to feel hopeful again and would follow wherever he led her.

They started up again, walking at random, simply to keep moving.

Gradually Becky grew tired, and had to sit down. Tom sat beside her and they began to talk of home, and friends, and comfortable beds. Becky cried, and Tom tried in vain to comfort her. Then she drowsed, and Tom was glad, and sat there watching over her. How long was it before she woke? However long it was, she was calmer, and anxious to look for a way out again. Hand in hand they set off, and when they reached a spring Tom said it was time to rest again.

Soon the candles flickered out and the horror of total darkness reigned. For hours they stayed where they were, in a stupor of weariness and despair.

Suddenly Tom thought he heard a noise. Perhaps someone was looking for them. He shook himself. There was a reel of kite-string in his pocket; he gave an end of it to Becky and set off down the side passage from which he thought the sound had come, undoing the reel and groping his way along.

As he was crawling forward, he suddenly saw a human figure holding a candle. Tom gave a shout of joy, but it died in his throat when he saw that the figure was that of Injun Joe!

Tom was paralysed, but he realised that his voice must have been disguised by the echo, and that Joe had dashed away.

Becky had noticed nothing and Tom was careful not to tell her what he had seen, and went back to explore another passage.

He was going down a long passage when he saw in the distance a luminous speck that might have been daylight. He ran towards it and the speck grew larger, until he discovered that the light was coming through a small hole; trembling with hope, he managed to push his head and shoulders through it, and the next minute he saw the Mississippi below him.

He rushed back to Becky and both ran back to the hole, where they pushed their way through and soon afterwards were sitting on the river bank. There they waited for a while till a skiff passed and they shouted to it.

The men took them on board, fed them and took them back to St. Petersburg.

Three days had passed since they had vanished in the cave, and all hope of finding them alive had been lost. The evening of their return was the happiest the village had ever known.

After the excitement and days of rest and recovery, Tom heard what had happened on Cardiff hill and went to look for Huck. But there was no sign of him, for after his adventure on the hill Huck had fallen ill, and the widow Douglas had taken him into her house, and forbidden all visitors.

It was a fortnight before Huck was better and Tom managed to see him. After this he went up to see Becky, and had a talk with Judge Thatcher, who asked him if he would like to go to the cave again.

When Tom said he would the Judge answered: "Well, no one will ever go there again. After you came back I had the big door covered with iron and triple locked, and I've got the keys."

Tom turned pale, then exclaimed, "Oh, Judge, Injun Joe's in the cave!"

Tom explained briefly, and in a few minutes skiffloads of men were on their way to the cave. When the door was unlocked, they found Injun Joe, starved to death, his face pressed to the crack of the door. His knife lay beside him; he had been trying to make a hole in the door with it, but had managed only a few small scratches. Tom was moved for he knew how the wretch had suffered, but at the same time felt a tremendous sense of relief that he no longer had to fear the evil man's vengeance.

After Injun Joe's burial Tom met Huck and felt it was time for revelations. He took him aside and said: "Huck, it's time for us to find the treasure. I know where 'number two' is. D'you want to come to the cave with me and help me?"

Tom and Huck rowed to the place where he and Becky had come back into daylight. It was not hard for the boys to get back into the cave and, with big candles, to find where Tom and Becky had been. After a while Tom said:

"Huck, look over there. That was where I saw Injun Joe. Do you think that must be 'number two'?"

Tom found footprints and some spots of candle grease, but only in a single place. Suddenly inspired, he started digging with the knife he had brought. Huck dug as well and a few inches below the surface they struck wood. Some boards were removed and showed a natural opening which led under the rock. Tom and Huck climbed down and found themselves in a small cave, in the middle of which stood the treasure-box.

They put the treasure into bags and carried it near widow Douglas's house; then they hurried inside. Waiting there they found not just the widow and Aunt Polly, but Judge Thatcher, the minister and other dignitaries. The widow had called a meeting to discuss her proposal to pay for Huck's education and put him on the way to earning a living.

When Tom heard what the good lady meant to do he exclaimed: "Huck doesn't need anything, because he's rich. I can show you!"

He ran out and reappeared carrying a large bag which he put on the table. Then he opened it and poured out the contents: a mass of gold coins.

"What did I tell you?" he asked the silent, astounded company. "Half of it's Huck's and half's mine!"

The money was counted and amounted to a little over twelve thousand dollars. Tom and Huck were rich. A new chapter was opening up in the two boys' lives, but would they have done without their adventures on the great river, their exciting games together? Certainly not!